Pinga'
Lost Rabbit

Pingu was teasing his little sister by copying her. He rocked his teddy and talked to it, just like Pinga with her rabbit.

Pinga hugged her rabbit harder and sulked.

Pingu laughed.
He grabbed Pinga's
rabbit and gave her
his teddy to play
with instead.

But Pinga jumped up and down on the teddy. She wanted her rabbit back.

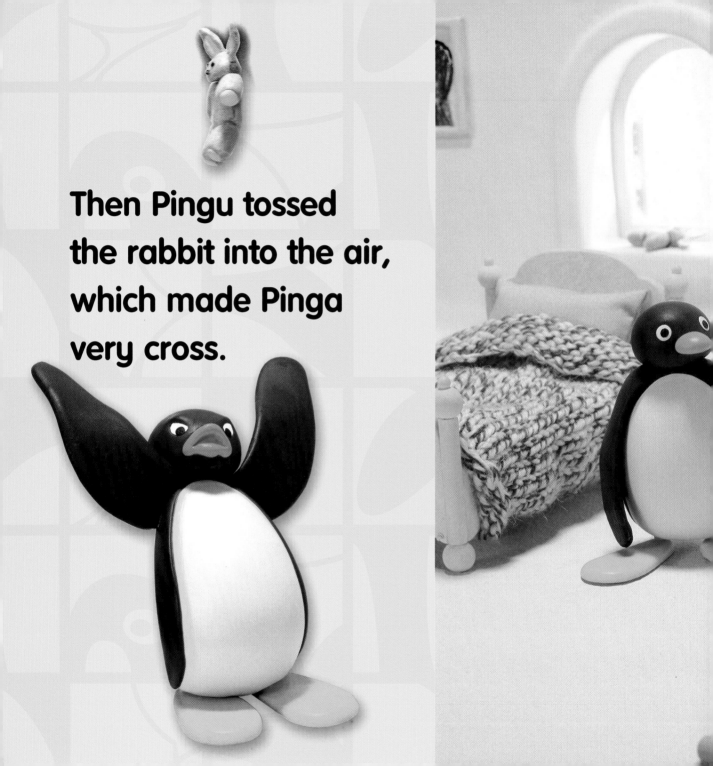

Then Pingu tossed
the rabbit into the air,
which made Pinga
very cross.

Mother arrived to see what all the noise was about.

Pinga pointed to her rabbit on the windowsill.

Mother told Pingu to go
and get it, while Father
gave Pinga a cuddle.

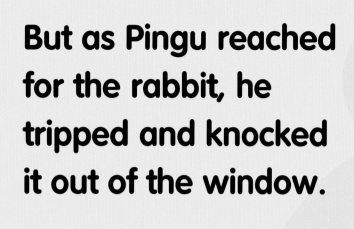
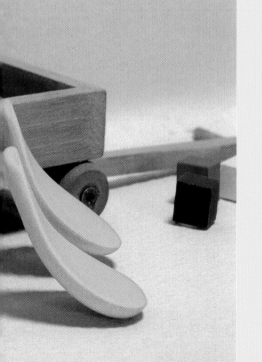

But as Pingu reached for the rabbit, he tripped and knocked it out of the window.

Father told Pingu to go and fetch it straight away!

Fed up, Pingu kicked
the rabbit and sent it
flying though the air.

It landed on the sledge, but then Pingu slipped on the ice...

...and the rabbit slid down
the hill.

It flew off the sledge, and
was caught by Robby.

Robby was having so much fun! But then he flipped the rabbit a bit too hard...

...and Pingu watched it fly far, far away...

...onto the middle of an iceberg. How would he ever reach it?

Luckily, there was
a fishing rod nearby.
Time for Pingu to test
his fishing skills.

Tired but happy, Pingu
finally returned home
with Pinga's rabbit.

Pinga, however, was more interested in playing with teddy.

Rabbit was left aside, as Pinga offered teddy more tea and cake.

Pingu couldn't believe it.
He picked up the rabbit
and put it on the chair.

Who would have thought a rabbit could cause so much trouble!